Moonlight Riders

ORCHARD BOOKS

First published in Great Britain in 2022 by Hodder & Stoughton Limited

1 3 5 7 9 10 8 6 4 2

Text copyright © Hodder & Stoughton Limited 2022
Illustrations copyright © Hodder & Stoughton Limited 2022
The moral rights of the author and illustrator have been asserted.

A CIP catalogue record for this book
is available from the British Library.

ISBN 978 1 40836 681 3

Printed and bound in Great Britain by Clays Ltd, Elcograf S.p.A.

The paper and board used in this book are made from wood from responsible sources.

FSC
www.fsc.org

MIX
Paper from
responsible sources
FSC® C104740

Orchard Books
An imprint of
Hachette Children's Group
Part of Hodder & Stoughton Limited
Carmelite House
50 Victoria Embankment
London EC4Y 0DZ

An Hachette UK Company
www.hachette.co.uk
www.hachettechildrens.co.uk

 # Contents

CHAPTER ONE

"There's a leak here! I need a bucket!" Amara shouted.

Kalini came splashing through the puddles, the hood of her coat pulled up to protect her from the rain that was cascading down from the grey sky. She thrust a bucket over Ember's stable door. "Here you go!"

"Thanks!" Amara said gratefully, grabbing the bucket and shoving it under the leak in Ember's roof.

It had been raining heavily for the last few days and when she and her friends, Kalini, Alex and Imogen, had arrived at the yard that morning, they had found Jill Reed, the owner of Moonlight Stables, trying to deal with leaks and overflowing water troughs.

Ember nuzzled Amara's plaits, water dripping from his coal-black forelock.

It's very wet in here! His mouth didn't move but Amara could hear his voice in her head. Ember, like the other nine beautiful ponies in the Meadow Stable block, was an elemental horse. Elemental horses were magic. They looked like regular ponies most of the time but they could transform into their true shape whenever they wanted to and they each had their own special powers. Ember was a Fire Horse who could make things burst into flame. Every elemental horse tried to find a True Rider – someone who would help them use their magic. Six weeks ago, Ember had chosen Amara. She still had to pinch herself sometimes to believe that it was real!

Can't you or one of the other horses do something to stop the rain, Ember? Amara asked.

He shook his head. *This rain is just normal rain. We're not supposed to use our elemental powers to interfere with natural weather events unless someone is in real danger.*

Amara hugged him. There was nothing she loved more than doing magic with Ember – it was amazing to feel the elemental energy rushing through him and into her. It made her feel as if every cell in her body was sparkling. *As soon as it stops raining, we'll have to go to the meadow with the others and practise magic some more,* she told him.

Ember snorted happily. *Definitely!*

Overhead the old roof timbers creaked.

Amara heard Imogen shout, "Hey, guys! Tide's stable has a massive leak!"

Amara left Ember and went to see if she could help. Water was pouring in through a large hole in Tide's stable roof. It had already filled the bucket that Imogen had put underneath it. Tide, a slim snow-white pony, was using her magical power over water to make the flood flow out of the stable door.

"I'll get a broom to help sweep the water out," said Kalini.

"I'll fetch a bucket!" said Amara.

"Or we could use this!" Alex said, grabbing a wheelbarrow from where it was leaning against the outside stable wall.

He pushed the wheelbarrow under the leak and the water splashed into it from the hole in the roof. "See. Much better than a bucket! I'm a genius!"

He turned and tripped over the bucket of water, spilling it everywhere.

Imogen rolled her eyes at him. "Some genius!" she grinned. She and Alex were great friends but they did like to wind each other up. "I'd better go and ask Jill if Tide can stay in one of the spare stables in the riding school block until this leak is fixed."

The horses and ponies that Jill used in the riding school were non-magical and they were kept in a separate, more modern stable block close to the driveway.

The roof creaked again – louder this time. Imogen stopped in her tracks.

"That doesn't sound good," said Kalini uneasily.

Amara frowned. "You don't think the roof is going to—" She was interrupted by a creaking, splintering noise overhead.

"The roof is caving in!" Imogen shrieked as tiles and bits of wood started to rain down around them.

"The ponies!" shouted Alex. "Get them out!"

Amara felt a rush of horror as she thought of roof beams falling on top of Ember and the other ponies, but just then there was a loud whinny from Rose in the stable next door. Suddenly a green blur rushed over their heads with a loud rustle of leaves.

Looking up, Amara saw there was now a thick blanket of vines and creepers knitting the broken beams together.

"What just happened?" said Kalini in astonishment.

"It was Rose!" Alex exclaimed. "She must

have used her magic to stop the roof from collapsing!"

He ran to the stable next door. Rose, his elemental horse, was a chestnut pony with a flaxen mane and tail. She was breathing fast. Using her earth magic to conjure the plants had clearly taken a lot of energy.

"You're the best, Rose," Alex said, hugging his pony. She raised her head and nuzzled his shoulder, her dark eyes pleased.

Amara heard Jill shouting their names and went to the stable door. Jill hobbled towards them through the rain on crutches. A week ago, she had broken her ankle falling down a step and she now had a large protective boot on and was having to use crutches to get around. "What's going on?" she demanded. "I heard an awful noise."

They quickly explained.

"Rose saved everyone by stopping the roof from caving in!" said Alex proudly.

"Clever pony. I'm so glad she thought to use her magic," said Jill.

When Jill was younger, she had been a True Rider but her horse, Shula, a Fire Horse like Ember, had died in an accident. Amara didn't know all the details – Jill didn't talk about it much, which Amara could completely understand. She didn't think she could bear it if anything happened to Ember. Imogen had told her that after Shula's accident, Jill had decided to make it her life's work to give other elemental horses a safe place to live and to help them find their True Riders.

"How long will it be before you can get the

roof fixed?" Kalini asked.

Jill rubbed her hands over her face, her blue eyes worried. "I don't know. I've had to cancel so many lessons recently because the rains flooded the school, so money's a bit tight. I can't even take riders out on extra hacks because of my ankle." She nodded at the big protective boot on her foot.

"If you can't get the roof repaired, what will the ponies in the Meadow Stables do?" asked Amara.

"I'll ask Rose to regrow the vines each day but doing that amount of magic will sap her strength so it's not a long-term solution."

"Could the ponies live outside?" Imogen suggested.

"Not while the weather is this bad," Jill replied. "The meadow is so muddy. They'll get mud fever on their legs if they are out for too long in it. It wouldn't be good at all. No, I'll have to find somewhere else for them to go."

"You mean take them to a different yard?" said Amara, her heart sinking. Her cottage was just down the road from Moonlight Stables and she loved being able to walk to see Ember whenever she wanted.

Jill sighed. "I doubt any yard will be able to take all nine ponies. If it gets to that point, they'll all have to go to separate yards."

There was an immediate outcry.

"Split up!"

"They can't! No way!"

"They've got to be together!"

"What about the mounted games squad?"

All the elemental horses were part of Jill's

mounted games squad – she believed games training was a great way for the ponies and their True Riders to develop their bond.

Jill held up her hands. "Look, it's not what I want either. Let's just hope the weather improves so I can give enough lessons to get the stable roof fixed – and keep Moonlight Stables going."

"What do you mean – keep Moonlight Stables going?" Amara asked.

"I'm sorry, everyone," Jill said heavily. "But if things don't improve, Moonlight Stables might have to close down."

CHAPTER TWO

"We need to come up with a plan!" hissed
Imogen as Jill hobbled away. "We can't let
the ponies be separated and we definitely –
definitely – can't let Moonlight Stables close.
Agreed?"

"Agreed!" they all echoed.

As soon as they had dried and fed the
ponies, they hurried to the tack room – an
old wooden building where the saddles
and bridles were kept along with the riding

helmets and grooming kits. It had a few leaks in its roof but Jill had plugged them with pieces of tarpaulin, and it was heated by a portable radiator so it was warm and cosy. There was a radio playing in the background, a kettle and a sink, and they made mugs of hot chocolate before sitting down on the two threadbare sofas.

"OK, how can we raise money to help Jill?" said Imogen, straightening her glasses and then going over to the radio to turn it off.

"Wait!" said Amara, her ears catching something. "Did the radio just say Storm Stables?"

Storm Stables was a very smart competition yard on the outskirts of town. It was the only other stable in Eastwall and was owned by Ivy Thornton, who was a

Night Rider – a True Rider who had turned bad. Night Riders used the elemental horses' powers for their own selfish gain.

Everyone fell quiet and listened.

"*Do you want to learn to ride at the best stables in Eastwall?*" Ivy's voice purred out of the radio as the advert for Storm Stables played. "*Then enrol at Storm Stables, where we offer state-of-the-art facilities, highly experienced trainers and the most accomplished horses. With a cross country course, dressage and showjumping arenas and not one, but two indoor schools, you'll never have to miss a riding session because of the weather.*" A musical jingle played and a voice sang: "*If you want to be the best, then ride with the best at . . . STORM STABLES!*"

They all swapped looks. "That advert

does make Storm Stables sound good," said Kalini.

"I heard Jill telling my dad the other day that since the school here has been flooded, quite a lot of the people who used to come for lessons have moved to Storm Stables," said Alex, looking serious for once.

"Poor Jill," said Imogen, shaking her head.

"Stupid people," said Amara crossly. "Ivy is so awful. Why can't they see that?"

"We really need to raise money to help Jill," said Imogen. "What can we do?"

"We could do a radio advert like Storm Stables," suggested Alex. "Or what about a TV advert? That would be even better!"

"It's much too expensive," said Imogen, shaking her head. "If Jill doesn't have the money to fix the stable roof, there's no way she'll have enough money to do a TV or even a radio advert."

"We need to think of a way to make money quickly for her," said Amara, "How about we give pony rides at the park?"

"Or we could do a bake sale and run a face painting stall to raise money," said Imogen.

"Or do a musical riding display to show how good the ponies are," said Kalini.

"Let's do everything!" declared Alex.

Imogen sighed. "Alex, be sensible. This is important."

"No, wait, Alex is right!" Amara said suddenly.

"See," Alex said smugly to Imogen, then he frowned at Amara. "How am I right?"

Her eyes shone with excitement. "If we had an open day here at the stables, then we could do all those things – pony rides, a cake stall, a face painting stall, a riding display – and it would mean we could raise money and advertise the yard at the same time—"

"And make everyone see how awesome Moonlight Stables is. Then they'll all want Jill to give them and their kids lessons," interrupted Alex. He high-fived Amara. "Awesome!"

"Wait," said Imogen suddenly. "I've thought of a problem."

Alex groaned. "Immy, why do you always think of problems?"

"Ssh, Alex. What is it?" Amara asked Imogen.

"Well, I know we all love this place and it's the best yard ever," said Imogen. "But it's not looking its best right now. Before we have an open day, maybe it would be best to help Jill tidy everywhere up – paint the stable doors and the fences, plant some flowers. That kind of thing."

"But that would cost money," Kalini pointed out.

"I know," said Imogen, chewing her lower

lip. "So, how about we raise some money before the open day? Maybe we could sell something?"

Kalini gasped. "Horse poo!"

"Horse poo?" Imogen echoed.

Alex huffed at her. "And you say *I'm* the one who's not sensible! Kalini, who'd pay for horse poo?"

"Gardeners," said Kalini triumphantly. "My grandpa always puts horse manure on his roses. He says it's a really good fertiliser. We could bag up the manure in old feed bags and take it into town to sell it. I bet we could earn enough money to buy some paint and things to make the yard look better."

Amara whooped. "That's a brilliant idea, Kalini! Let's ask Jill right now!"

Jill was very surprised when they told her
their ideas and she even started to look
a little emotional. "You are all so lovely,
wanting to help out like this. Of course you
can raise some money by selling fertiliser,
and we can have an open afternoon. The
trouble is, I'm not going to be much use with
this on," she said, pointing at the boot on her
foot.

"Don't worry, we'll do everything," Alex
said. "We can get Ollie, Jasmine and Bea to
help too." They were the other three riders
on the mounted games squad. Jasmine
and Ollie were both fourteen; Jasmine was
Cloud's True Rider and Ollie was Sirocco's.

They couldn't spend as much time at the stables as they would like to because they had a lot of schoolwork now they were in Year Nine. Bea was nine, two years younger than Amara. She rode Sandy and everyone thought she would one day become Sandy's True Rider but it hadn't happened yet.

Amara, Kalini, Alex and Imogen fetched a load of old paper feed sacks and put gloves on. The ponies watched curiously as they

shovelled manure inside the sacks, carefully tying the tops with twine. Luckily the rain had stopped and there were even a few patches of blue sky between the grey clouds.

"How are we going to get the bags into town?" asked Kalini. "Jill can't drive because of her foot."

Imogen pulled a face. "I can't see any of our mums or dads wanting to put bags of horse manure in their cars."

"My dad might let us put them in his van," suggested Amara. Her dad ran his own property maintenance company. "But he's out working today."

Rose whinnied and Alex looked at her. "Yes! That's it, Rose!"

"What did Rose say?" asked Imogen.

"There's a cart in the barn that Rose has

been trained to pull. If we put the sacks on that, she said she can pull the cart up the High Street."

"Perfect!" said Amara in delight. "I bet loads of people will come out when they see a horse and cart."

They checked it was OK with Jill and then they heaved the old cart out of the barn and fetched the harness from the tack room. They dusted off the cobwebs and loaded the bags on to the back, then Rose stamped her front hoof. White roses appeared, decorating the cart.

"Oh, Rose, that looks great!" said Amara.

Rose whinnied smugly then tossed her mane, making her harness jingle.

Alex jumped on to the driver's seat. "Let's go and raise us some money!"

CHAPTER THREE

They headed up the lane that led to the stables and then turned on to the High Street. They'd made a big poster that said *FERTILISER £1 A BAG*. Rose whinnied loudly, drawing people out of the houses and shops.

"Come and buy some fertiliser. It's for a good cause!" called Amara, rattling the tin and thoroughly enjoying the stares and smiles as children pointed at Rose. "We're raising money for Moonlight Stables!"

"All natural and great for the garden. One pound a bag!" shouted Imogen.

Kalini took people's money while Alex unloaded the bags from the back of the cart. The pound coins rattled into the tin they were using to collect the money and the bags gradually went down in number. Amara was delighted. This was going better than they could ever have imagined!

They were down to their last few bags when a woman dressed in a sleeveless green padded jacket and long brown country boots approached them. "What a beautiful pony," she said, stroking Rose. Rose whickered and nuzzled her. "Where are you all from?"

"Moonlight Stables," chorused Amara, Imogen and Kalini.

"The best riding school around," Alex added.

"And are all the ponies as well behaved as this one?" asked the woman.

"Absolutely," said Kalini.

"I see." The woman nodded thoughtfully. "And can this pony and cart be hired out?"

"You'd have to speak to Jill, who owns the stables," said Imogen. "But I imagine she'd be happy to help. I can give you her number if you'd like."

"Yes, please."

"I wonder what that was about?" Amara said, puzzled, after the woman walked off.

Before Imogen had a chance to reply, they heard a familiar voice. "Oh my goodness! Look, Daniela, the Moonlight Stables losers are selling horse poo!"

Heart sinking, Amara turned and saw two girls dressed in very smart riding clothes approaching them. It was Zara and Daniela – two of her least favourite people in the world. They were cousins and had once been riders at Moonlight Stables. Zara had ridden Ember but when he had chosen Amara to be his True Rider, she had left in a huff and made Daniela go with her. They now rode with Ivy at Storm Stables.

Zara's pale blue eyes glinted. "I have got to take a picture of this," she said, pulling out her phone.

Daniela smirked. "Things must be really bad at Moonlight Stables."

"Oh, go away, you two!" said Alex crossly.

"Ivy told us that Jill's been losing all her clients," said Daniela.

"What a shame, Moonlight Stables might have to shut down," said Zara, not sounding like she thought it was a shame at all. "Well, don't come running to Storm Stables when it does."

"As if we would," said Amara.

"Yeah," muttered Alex crossly. "It's the last place we'd ever go!" He was in the middle of trying to lift a bag of fertiliser down from the cart but it had got caught on the corner of one of the seats.

"Do you want a hand?" Amara asked him.

"No, I'm fine," he said, tugging at the bag.

"Here, let me help—" Amara began but it was too late. Alex had pulled so hard that the paper sack had ripped. With a gasp, he staggered backwards, spilling fertiliser all over himself.

Zara and Daniela hooted with laughter as Alex stood there with manure splattered around his feet. Zara turned to the watching crowd and smirked. "If you want to ride and

win, come to Storm Stables," she called out.
"But if you want to smell like poo, Moonlight
Stables is the place for you!"

She and Daniela walked off sniggering.

A kind shopkeeper brought out a broom
and a damp cloth for Alex to wipe himself
down with. After Amara and the others had
cleared up the mess, they sold the last bag
of fertiliser and headed home. "Zara and
Daniela are so annoying!" said Amara.

"Storm Stables is so cool," said Alex,
mimicking Zara's snooty voice. *"We're all so
great."*

"Let's not talk about them," said Imogen.
"The important thing is we sold all the
fertiliser."

"And raised lots of money!" said Kalini,
shaking the full tin. "Well, enough to get

started on the clean-up anyway."

When they got back, Jill met them on the driveway. She was looking pleased. "I just had a phone call from a lady called Mrs Patterson. She said she met you on the High Street and she was very impressed by how polite you were and how well behaved Rose was. She's organising an event at Brookston Agricultural College next Saturday and she was wondering if we'd like to take Rose and her cart along as well as a couple of the ponies to give pony rides. She said we can charge people and keep any money we make. She just wants there to be as many fun activities at the event as possible. When I told her I can't drive, she even offered to get someone to drive over in one of the college horse lorries to pick the ponies and cart up.

It sounds like a great idea – are any of you free to help out so I can say yes?"

Amara swapped excited looks with the others. It sounded like a brilliant way to make some more money! "I'm free. I can help."

"Me too," said Kalini. Alex and Imogen nodded as well.

"We can print out posters and leaflets advertising our open afternoon and hand them out while we're there," said Imogen eagerly.

"Great idea! I'll ring Jasmine, Ollie and Bea to see if they'll help too," said Jill.

Amara's tummy fizzed with happiness as she ran to the Meadow Stable block. Seeing her coming, Ember whinnied in delight. *Did you raise much money?* he asked as she opened his stable door and hugged him.

Amara told him everything that had happened – and about the event the following weekend.

I'll give pony rides, Ember offered.

Amara looked at him in surprise. Elemental horses usually only wanted their True Riders to ride them. *Really? We can use the riding school ponies.*

But if it's dry, Jill will need them for

lessons. And I'd really like to help. Ember nudged her with his nose.

All right, but are you sure you'll be OK with little children riding you? Amara tried to be tactful. *I mean, you can be quite lively . . .*

I'll be good as gold, Ember promised.

"Ember wants to give pony rides at the college next weekend," Amara called to the others, who were fussing their ponies.

"So does Tide!" said Imogen.

"Thunder's offered as well," said Kalini.

Amara beamed. Although the riding school ponies were all very cute, the elemental horses were strikingly beautiful. They would be a brilliant advert for Moonlight Stables and hopefully encourage lots of people to come to the open afternoon.

If we can make the yard look great and we do a really good musical display ride, then maybe, just maybe, Jill will get lots more clients signing up for lessons and won't have to shut down, Amara thought.

Determination filled her. She would do everything she could to make that happen!

CHAPTER FOUR

The week passed quickly. Rose used her
magic every day to keep the temporary roof
in place and luckily the weather improved.
The puddles in the school drained away
and Jill was able to book in lessons for the
weekend.

Imogen, who was the best at art, designed
a poster advertising the open afternoon
and Alex's mum printed out lots of copies.
They met in the High Street after school

on Wednesday and attached some to lamp posts as well as going round all the shops asking if they could put the posters up in their windows. Nearly all the shopkeepers said yes and some of them even promised to come along. Everything seemed to be going according to plan.

On Saturday, they got to the stables early to bathe the ponies. They wanted them to look their very best when they gave pony rides! Ember helped by using his magic to heat the water in the trough up and then Tide used her powers to make the water spiral into the air and rain down in warm droplets. Amara and the others got busy rubbing the shampoo in and then Ember and Tide repeated the process to wash away the suds and leave their coats sparkling clean.

Thunder and Sirocco used their powers to blow dry all the ponies.

"Who needs hoses and buckets when you've got elemental horses," said Alex, chuckling at the fluffy quiff Sirocco had given Rose.

By the time the horse lorry arrived, the four ponies were gleaming, the saddles and bridles were lined up on the fence and the cart and harness had been decorated by Rose

with bright spring flowers. Amara noticed that Rose wasn't looking quite her normal self. Her eyes didn't have their usual sparkle and her coat looked duller.

"Is Rose OK?" she asked Alex.

A look of concern crossed Alex's face. "I think that using her magic each day to regrow the roof is tiring her out."

"We should have used ribbons to decorate the cart instead of flowers," said Amara, feeling guilty. "When is the next moonlight ritual?"

During the first full moon at the start of each new season, the ponies could restore their magic by going for a gallop in the moonlight. Alex shook his head. "Not until June."

"That's weeks away," said Amara.

Alex nodded. "I hope she's going to be OK."

Looking at Rose as she rested one hind leg, her head hanging low, Amara really hoped so too.

When the Moonlight Stables ponies arrived at Brookston College, the grounds were bustling with people. Some were setting up stalls and refreshment vans; others were putting out seating around the main arena where there would be riding displays and parades of farm animals throughout the day. Jasmine, Ollie and Bea met Amara and the others there and they all set to work, putting out a table where they would take the money, arranging cushions in the cart, lining up a row of hats for the children having pony rides to wear, grooming the ponies and knocking a sign that Jill had made into the ground:

Moonlight Stables
Pony rides: £1 per person
Pony and cart rides around the
showground: £2 per person

As Amara gave the ponies a final polish, she noticed a tall, slim girl watching her. She looked about thirteen and was wearing old joggers and a baggy grey hoodie. Her dark hair was tied back in a low ponytail.

Amara smiled. "Hi."

The girl gave Amara a quick, shy smile back and turned away.

"Wait, you don't have to go," called Amara. She could vividly remember how shy she used to feel around ponies before she had found Moonlight Stables and become Ember's rider. Every time she had seen a pony, she had longed to go close to it and stroke it. Maybe this girl felt the same.

"Our ponies are all really friendly," she said. "You can stroke them if you want."

The girl came over. "They're beautiful," she

said, patting Ember.

Amara beamed. "Thanks! Would you like to help me groom them?"

The girl hesitated then shrugged. "OK." Amara wondered if she would have to show

her what to do
but when she
handed the girl
a body brush,
it was clear
straight away she
knew how to use
it, sweeping it
over Tide's coat
with confident
strokes.

"We're from
Moonlight

Stables," Amara said to her. She wondered if the girl might be a potential new client. "Do you ride?"

The girl nodded.

"We're having an open afternoon next weekend. You should come along," said Amara brightly. "We're trying to raise money – one of our stable blocks has got a hole in its roof." She chattered on about Moonlight Stables as they brushed the ponies. The girl didn't say much but Amara noticed that Tide and the other ponies seemed to like her. They all nuzzled her affectionately as she brushed them. She helped Amara put hoof oil on all of them and then the loudspeaker crackled. "The gates will be opening in five minutes!" the announcer called.

"I'd better go," the girl said. "I hope you

raise lots of money today."

"Thanks!" Amara said. The girl hurried off, the gates opened and soon the ponies were surrounded by children all wanting to pat them and have a ride. While Jasmine and Bea took the money and handed out posters for the open day, Ollie helped fit helmets and then Amara, Imogen and Kalini led the children up and down the field on Ember, Tide and Thunder. Meanwhile, Alex and Rose gave people rides around the field in the cart.

The ponies seemed to love all the fuss. However, after a while Amara could tell Ember was getting bored with walking up and down the same bit of the field. On their tenth journey, he mischievously stamped his hoof and fiery sparks flew up from the ground. The little girl on his back gasped. "What was that?"

"Nothing," said Amara, shooting a look at Ember. *Stop it!* she told him with her thoughts.

Why? It's fun! he said, giving her a cheeky look. He tapped one hoof lightly on the ground again. A tiny spark appeared, fading almost instantly. The girl gasped and when Amara helped her down, she raced to her mum.

"Mummy! Mummy! That pony made sparks fly from his hooves!"

Her mum smiled. "Did he really, Elsie? Wow!" she said, clearly not believing it.

"My pony made a puddle split in half so it could walk through it!" called the girl's sister, who had been riding Tide.

"What clever ponies!" their mum chuckled.

"Can we go to this riding school when we start riding lessons? Please!" begged Elsie as Thunder got back with his rider – a little boy.

"You should come along to our open day," Imogen said quickly. "Jill, our riding teacher, is great. There are some leaflets on the table." The girls pulled their mum over to the table to get a leaflet. The boy who had been riding Thunder dismounted and ran over as well, his mum following.

Amara turned to Tide and Ember. "Stop it, you two!" she whispered. "We can't let anyone see you doing magic, remember!"

Ember blinked at her innocently. *Magic? I don't know what you mean, Amara?*

Tide's eyes sparkled. She stamped a hoof and the water in a nearby water bucket shot up into the air in a straight, glittering column. Unfortunately, at the same moment, the boy's mum glanced towards them. Seeing the column of water shooting magically into the sky, her eyes widened in astonishment. "Oh my!" she exclaimed.

"Quick!" Amara squeaked to the horses. "Do something!"

CHAPTER FIVE

Thunder stamped his front hooves down and a strong wind instantly swirled up. It scattered the column of water into millions of droplets and at the same time sent the leaflets advertising the stables flying up from the table. They danced around in the breeze. The children laughed and tried to catch them while their parents, Jasmine, Ollie and Bea all joined in.

After a few minutes, Thunder let the wind

drop and order was quickly restored. The parents and their children helped pick up the leaflets and put the ones that weren't too muddy back in a pile on the table. Imogen put all the ruined leaflets in the bin. The little boy's mum looked at where the column of water had been.

"Mummy, I want an ice cream!" her son said, tugging at her hand.

His mum gave a shake of her head as if

telling herself she must have imagined it. "Thanks for the pony ride!" she called as she let him pull her away. "We'll definitely come along to the open day."

"Tide! No more magic!" hissed Imogen.

"You too, Ember!" said Amara.

OK, he said. He gave her a cheeky look. *It was lots of fun though!*

After an hour, the girls and Alex gave the ponies a break. They tied them up beside the horsebox so they could graze. "I'm starving!" said Alex. "Can we get something to eat?"

Jasmine and Ollie had brought sandwiches with them and said they were happy to stay and keep an eye on the ponies while the others found some food. There was a hot dog van near the main ring where the displays were taking place. They all bought hot dogs and drinks and wandered over to the ring to see what was going on. A rectangular dressage arena was being set up inside the ring – around the edges there were pots of flowers and white boards with letters on them.

The loudspeaker crackled. "Our next display will take us to the elegant world of dressage . . . "

Alex groaned. "I'm not watching dressage – it's really boring!"

"I like dressage," Imogen said.

"Me too," said Kalini.

Amara didn't really know anything about dressage but she did love the way that dressage horses looked like they were dancing when they were doing their routines to music.

"We're very lucky to have a bright, young local dressage star who has come here today fresh from competing in – and winning – her first international competition," said the announcer. "Please welcome Malia Talab riding the beautiful Parkway Golden Sands!"

Everyone around the ring clapped. Amara joined in, expecting to see an adult rider coming into the ring but instead it was a girl a little older than her riding a stunning palomino pony whose coat gleamed like gold. The girl wore white breeches, a smart navy coat with gold buttons and long black boots. Her dark hair was tucked into a hairnet under her hat. She rode the pony in

a circle outside the boards and then, as the music started, she turned up the centre line. Seeing her face properly, Amara gasped. It was the girl she had met earlier!

Kalini realised it too. "Isn't that the girl who was helping you groom the ponies?"

"Yeah," said Amara. "I asked her if she could ride and she said yes. She didn't say she was a superstar dressage rider though!"

They watched in awe as Malia and her pony performed the complicated dressage test in perfect time to the music. Even though Amara didn't know much about dressage, it was clear to her that Malia and her pony shared just as close a bond as the True Riders all did with their elemental horses.

The routine finished and the audience erupted into applause. Malia bowed, her cheeks flushed, and then she loosened her reins, patted her pony's neck and rode out of the arena.

"Let's go and say well done!" said Amara.

Throwing their hot dog wrappers in a bin, they hurried around the outside of the ring to where Malia was dismounting. There was a small group of people around her. A woman dressed in smart jeans and long brown boots, who looked as if she might be Malia's mum, was talking to a reporter from the local paper while the paper's photographer took some snaps of Malia and her pony. Now she was no longer riding, Malia's confidence seemed to have vanished. She muttered brief answers to the interviewer's questions, looking as if she would rather be anywhere else.

"And what school do you go to, Malia?" the reporter asked.

"Malia's home educated," her mum answered for her. "It means we can keep up with her training."

Malia caught sight of Amara and for a brief moment, a smile lit up her face.

But then a sharp voice cut through the air. "Malia, darling! You were wonderful, simply wonderful!"

Amara saw Ivy Thornton, the owner of Storm Stables, heading towards them. Zara, Daniela and a third girl who Amara recognised as Shannon, another Storm Stables rider, were with her.

"Malia, you were fab!" said Zara, flinging her arms round her.

Malia shrank away from her.

"Just awesome!" said Shannon, giving her a big fake smile as she tucked her arm through Malia's and smiled straight at the camera. The photographer started taking a few more snaps.

"We're Malia's best friends," Daniela told the reporter, making sure she got into the pictures too.

"Malia has just moved her pony to my stables – Storm Stables," Ivy told the reporter. "Make sure that goes in your article!"

Amara felt Imogen tug at her sleeve. "I didn't realise Malia was at Storm Stables," Imogen hissed.

"Or that she was friends with that lot!" muttered Alex. "Come on, let's go."

Amara glanced at Malia. "I don't think she

is friends with them," she whispered. "Not really." The photographer put his camera away and almost instantly the other girls let go of Malia's arms and walked off together, leaving Malia on her own.

Ivy clicked her fingers and a smartly dressed groom with a Storm Stables shirt came over. "Take this pony back to the lorry," Ivy ordered.

"It's OK, I'll sort Goldie out . . . " Malia started to say.

Ivy shook her head. "Absolutely not! That's the groom's job – they're employed to look after the horses." She smiled broadly at Malia's mum. "Now, why don't the three of us go and get a drink in the café? I've reserved an area for VIPs only."

Malia's mum nodded and they walked off

together. Malia glanced back wistfully at her pony, who was being led away by the groom.

"Poor Malia," said Amara.

Imogen frowned. "What do you mean, poor Malia? She's really lucky. She's got a gorgeous pony, she doesn't have to go to school and she gets to compete around the world."

"But what about just grooming your pony, going for a hack, hanging out with your friends?" said Amara.

"You're right," said Kalini, linking arms with her. "I wouldn't swap what we have for anything."

When they got back to their stall, they found a queue of people waiting for the ponies. The money rattled into the tin and by the time they finished it was full of coins.

The gang were washing the ponies down when Malia appeared. She was dressed in her hoodie and tracksuit bottoms again.

"Hi," she said shyly.

"Hi," Amara said, giving her a friendly smile. "Your display was great."

Malia blushed. "Thanks. I'm really lucky to have Goldie – my pony – she's brilliant." She patted Ember's damp neck. "How did the pony rides go?"

"Really well," said Amara happily. "We made lots of money. Enough to buy paint for the stables anyway."

"Cool," said Malia.

"Amara!" Hearing Alex call her name, Amara turned. "Catch!" he yelled with a laugh as he threw a wet sponge straight at her face.

She squealed and dodged just in time. The sponge flew past her shoulder and hit Malia on the chin. She gasped in shock.

"Alex, you doughnut!" cried Imogen.

Alex looked horrified. "I'm sorry!" he said, running over. "I meant to get Amara. I didn't mean to hit *you!* I really am sor—" He broke off with a yell of surprise as Malia grinned, grabbed the sponge from the ground and chucked it back at him. It splatted into his chest.

"Water fight!" Alex yelled in glee.

The next moment, all the sponges were flying through the air and they were squealing and laughing as they ducked and dodged. Malia joined in, throwing the sponges with an extremely accurate aim. They continued until there was no water

left in the buckets and then collapsed on the damp grass together, laughing.

"Malia!"

Amara sat up as Malia's mum came walking towards them. She looked astonished to see Malia on the ground.

"I've got to go!" Malia said hastily, jumping to her feet and brushing the grass and mud off her joggers. "Bye!"

Everyone called goodbye as Malia ran over to her mum.

"She seems really nice," said Kalini.

"And not a bit stuck-up," agreed Alex. "Not

like someone from Storm Stables at all."

"I wonder if she'd do a dressage display at our open afternoon," said Amara thoughtfully, but then she shook her head. "No, I bet Ivy wouldn't let her even if she wanted to."

"You know, we'd better get started on our musical display," said Imogen. "It has to be good enough to make all the people watching decide they want Jill to teach them and their children to ride."

"We'll practise every night this week," said Kalini.

The others nodded. "This open afternoon is going to be a huge success!" declared Alex.

"It has to be!" Amara said. She couldn't bear the thought of Moonlight Stables having to close!

CHAPTER SIX

The next day, the clean-up of the yard started in earnest. While Jill was busy giving lessons in the morning, Amara and the rest of the mounted games squad set about sweeping the yard and feed room, scrubbing the stables and pulling up the weeds that seemed to be sprouting from every crack and crevice.

When the lessons finished and the last customer had left the yard, the ponies joined in with the clearing up. Rose and Cloud went with Alex and Jasmine to fill the empty plant pots and hanging baskets while Ember, Tide, Thunder, Sirocco, Forest and Sandy tackled the patches of nettles and brambles that were growing around the school.

This is fun! Ember said to Amara, stamping his foot and making a bramble bush erupt into flames.

Amara was riding him bareback – elemental horses always found it easier to do magic if their True Rider was with them. She could feel the magic surging through him. It made every centimetre of her skin feel like it was tingling.

You're so much better at controlling your magic than you used to be, she told him proudly. When Ember had first started using magic, he had struggled to control the fires he made.

That's because I've got you helping me, he said. The flames of the burning bush blazed up, sending a wave of heat towards them. Ember stamped his foot and they instantly died down again. He whinnied to Tide, who made water from the nearby trough shoot up into the sky and then curve down to hit the fire. The flames sizzled out in a cloud of smoke and then Thunder and Sirocco conjured up winds to sweep the smoke away, and Sandy covered the bare soil with a layer of sand to stop the weeds sprouting again. Forest attempted to grow some rose bushes but although he tried hard, he only managed to make a single, rather small rose grow. He was still very young and he didn't have much

control of his magic yet.

When they finished, Amara went to see how Alex and Jasmine were getting on. To her surprise, she found them sitting with Jill, transferring flowers by hand from plastic trays into empty pots. Cloud was watering the containers but Rose was just watching. She looked unhappy and Amara noticed again how dull her coat looked.

"Why isn't Rose using her magic?" Amara asked curiously.

"Rose is tired from having to use her magic every day to keep the roof in place," Jill said. "So I decided it would be best if she didn't help with the plant pots as well. Elemental horses get sick if they do too much magic. Your dad picked up some flowers from the garden centre when he got the paint for us this morning. He dropped everything off half an hour ago."

"Rose will be OK, won't she?" asked Amara, looking anxiously at the chestnut pony.

Jill nodded. "She'll be able to renew her magic at the next full moon."

"I wish it wasn't so long until then," said Alex, ruffling Rose's mane. "Isn't there anything else we can do to help her?"

Jill shook her head. "Not really. There is a magic spring on Magpie Hill that can renew elemental horses' magic – but it's several hours' ride away and dangerous to get to. The spring emerges halfway down a cliff that plunges into a deep ravine. I don't think it's worth the risk. Rose should be fine provided we look after her carefully and she only uses her magic once a day to renew the roof."

They spent the afternoon painting the stable doors. Each of the doors in the main stable block was painted a different pastel colour and Imogen painted each pony's name on in her best handwriting. They really brightened the stables up.

Leaving the paint to dry, Amara, Kalini, Imogen, Alex and Bea saddled their ponies up. The squad usually had a games practice on Sunday afternoon but Jill had agreed they could miss it so that they could work on the musical display instead. They'd worked out what they were going to do in it over lunch.

Jasmine and Ollie couldn't take part – they had exams that week and they knew they wouldn't be able to come to any practices – but they were still going to help out at the open afternoon. Ollie had offered to run a cake stall – he loved baking – and Jasmine had said she would get some friends from school to help with a face painting and hair braiding stall. They also both offered to fill some more sacks with fertiliser to sell.

When the rest of them all gathered in the school for their first practice, Alex made an announcement. "I've decided I'm not going to be in the display either."

"But Alex, you're one of our best riders," protested Imogen.

Alex patted Rose. "Thanks, but Rose is pretty tired from doing magic every day and I don't want to make her worse by riding her lots."

They all nodded, understanding. Their ponies' well-being always came first.

"I'll do the music and be in charge of the

practices," said Alex. He grinned. "It'll be fun bossing you lot around and I've thought of some cool extra things to add in!"

Soon they were trotting and cantering around in pairs while Alex stood with Rose in the middle and shouted instructions at them, telling them when to change direction

and change pace. Then they joined up and rode as a four. They were so used to working together as a mounted games squad and they all had such a good bond with their ponies that they found it easy to keep in time with each other. Alex whooped and clapped as they finished. "It's looking amazing already! The audience are going to love it. Now we just need to add the other riders in."

The six riding school ponies were all going to be in the display with riders from the riding school who were between six and ten years old.

"Will they manage OK? The riders on Pippin, Blue, Bella and Pepper are quite young and have only just come off the lead rein," said Kalini. "Some of the bits you just added in are pretty tricky."

"They'll be fine!" Alex said airily.

"But they won't be able to do all the moves at a canter like we can," said Imogen.

"They can just trot then," said Alex.

"Maybe we should have said we only wanted experienced riders for the display," said Imogen.

"No," said Alex. We want people to see that every rider's important at Moonlight Stables, not just the really good riders."

Amara nodded. "Yeah. We're not Storm Stables."

Imogen smiled. "Definitely not. OK, we'll keep the little ones in the display then."

"We're going to practise every night this week," said Alex. "So by Saturday the display will be perfect. You'll see!"

Unfortunately, things didn't go quite to

plan. Although Amara, Alex, Kalini, Imogen and Bea turned up every night to practise, all the other riders had after-school clubs and activities and they each only managed to come once or twice. The first night everyone was able to practise together was Friday – the night before the open day. It was a disaster!

The four youngest riders, Josh, Nikita, Cleo and Taylor, who had been paired up together, kept forgetting what to do and even when they did remember, they couldn't get their ponies to do what they wanted. They kept bumping into each other and giggling.

"Come on, guys!" Alex said, looking stressed. "Try and remember what I've told you! Look, I'll lead Pippin and Bella. Taylor and Nikita, you follow on Pepper and Blue."

But Pepper decided she wasn't going

to move no matter how hard Taylor used her legs and Blue walked off in the wrong direction.

"He won't turn, Alex!" shouted Nikita, pulling on the reins frantically.

Amara could see Alex was close to losing his temper. She jumped off Ember. "Hey, Alex, why don't I help you?"

"I'll give you a hand too," said Imogen, dismounting.

"No," Alex said, shaking his head. "I need you two to stay as a pair and lead the ride."

"Kalini and Bea can do that. The younger ones will get the hang of it all more quickly if we help," said Imogen.

"No! I don't need help!" Alex said crossly.

Amara and Imogen exchanged looks but, not wanting to make Alex even more cross, they remounted. They started the display again from the beginning with Alex running between the four younger ones. Taylor, Nikita, Cleo and Josh tried to do what he said but they kept getting muddled up and their ponies were easily distracted.

"I wish Alex would let us help him," Amara whispered to Imogen.

"I know!" said Imogen. "He's so stubborn!"

"What are we going to do?" Amara said.

"We're having another practice in the morning," said Imogen. "If they can't remember it then we'll just have to suggest they do the beginning bit with us – the easy bit – and then halt in the middle while we do the rest."

Amara nodded. It wasn't a great solution – it would look so much better if all the riders did the whole ride – but she could see that it might be the only solution.

After the practice, she took Ember down to the meadow for a graze. *Oh Ember*, she said, stroking him. *I hope the display isn't a disaster.*

It won't be, he told her.

She put her arms round his neck and breathed in his sweet, comforting smell.

By this time tomorrow, it'll all be over, he told her.

I really want it to go well, she said.

Me too, but whatever happens we'll still have each other. Ember lifted his muzzle to her face.

She kissed his soft nose. He was right but she couldn't help worrying about what they'd do if they didn't make enough money to save the stables. She knew her parents couldn't afford for her to keep a pony at another yard. If Moonlight Stables shut, would she be separated from Ember for ever?

CHAPTER SEVEN

Amara had invited Kalini to stay at her house that night. "I thought we'd get a takeaway for tea," Amara's dad said when they got in from the stables. "It's just the three of us eating tonight." Amara's mum taught at Eastwall Academy – the local secondary school – and had a parents' evening. "How does fish and chips sound?"

"Yummy!" said Amara. She loved chips from the chip shop. "But ..."

"Yep, sausage and chips for you," her dad said, tweaking one of her plaits. "How about you, Kalini?"

"Fishcakes and chips, please," she said.

"Great. Go and wash your hands and then I'll whizz us up there in the van."

"We can check all our posters are still up while Dad's getting the food," Amara said to Kalini as they ran upstairs.

Amara's dad parked near the fish and chip shop. As the girls were getting out of the van, they saw Ivy Thornton pulling down a poster they had attached to a lamp post. She crumpled it up angrily and then marched back to her sports car, scowling. Throwing the balled-up poster inside the car, she drove off in a screech of tyres.

"That's so mean!" said Kalini.

"I hope the other posters are still up," said Amara, feeling worried.

While Amara's dad stood in the queue at the chip shop, the girls checked all the shop windows. They were relieved to see that the other posters they had put up inside the shops were still on display.

"Hi."

Hearing a familiar voice, Amara looked round and saw Malia. "Hey, Malia!" she said, giving her a friendly smile.

"How's Goldie?" asked Kalini. "And Storm Stables?"

"Goldie's fine but . . . " Malia's face fell. "Storm Stables . . . well . . . " She bit her lip. "I don't like it!" Her words came out in a rush.

Amara and Kalini exchanged looks.

"I don't like the people," Malia said

miserably. "There's these girls – Zara, Shannon and —"

"Daniela. Yeah, we know them," said Amara.

"They're so mean," said Malia. "I wish I could keep Goldie at your stables. I asked my mum but she said I need to be somewhere with an indoor school so I can ride all year."

"Malia?" Malia's mum came out of the takeaway shop and walked over to them holding a bag of fish and chips.

"This is Amara and Kalini, Mum. They're from Moonlight Stables," Malia said. "I helped with their ponies at the college event."

"Oh, yes, I remember," her mum said, giving them a quick smile. "You were giving pony rides to raise money for your stables."

Amara nodded. "We're having an open afternoon tomorrow too," she said. She pointed to the notice in the Post Office window. "If you're free, why don't you come along? It starts at two o'clock. There will be lots of fun things to do."

Malia turned to her mum. "Can we?"

"If you want," her mum said.

"You could help us get ready, Malia," Amara said impulsively. "There'll be loads to do."

Malia's mum smiled. "That's very nice of you, Amara, but Malia's quite shy and I don't think she'll want to—"

"I do want to!" Malia interrupted.

Her mum looked surprised. "Oh ... well, OK. What time should Malia arrive?"

"Any time," said Amara. "Kalini and I are

meeting the others at the stables at six-thirty so any time after that."

"I'll drop her off after breakfast then," her mum said with a smile.

"See you tomorrow!" Malia said happily.

"I can't believe you asked Malia to our open day!" Kalini said as Malia and her mum got into a very smart sports car and drove off. "She's an international dressage rider!"

"I know, but it sounds like she's having a rubbish time at Storm Stables." A thought struck Amara and her eyes widened. "Maybe she'll be able to persuade her mum to let her keep Goldie with us!"

Kalini shook her head. "You heard what she said. We haven't got an indoor school."

"Oh yeah," said Amara, remembering. "It's a pity. It would be much nicer for Malia than being at Storm Stables."

Kalini linked arms with her. "Well, maybe after tomorrow Jill will get so many new customers that she'll be able to build an indoor school!"

Even in Amara's wildest dreams she knew that was unlikely to happen. She sighed. "I just want Jill to be able to keep Moonlight Stables open."

"Me too," Kalini agreed fervently. "I hate the thought of us having to go to different stables."

"Or not being able to keep Ember and Thunder at all," said Amara, remembering what she'd been thinking about back at the stables.

Amara's dad came out of the chip shop. "Food!" he called, waving the bag at them.

Breathing in a waft of the delicious smell of freshly cooked chips, Amara pushed down her worries and ran with Kalini to join her dad.

The next morning, Amara woke up just as dawn was breaking. She sat up in bed, feeling that something was horribly wrong. She drew her knees up to her chest. Maybe she'd just been having a bad dream? She waited for a few minutes to see if she felt better but the feeling of dread needling down her spine grew stronger. Kalini stirred uneasily on the camp bed and muttered something in her sleep. Throwing back the covers, Amara went to her bedroom window. She caught her breath as a bolt of white lightning suddenly forked down through the sky. Ivy's elemental horse, Bolt, was able to control lightning.

Fear stabbed through her. Was something magical going on?

"Kalini!" she hissed, running over and shaking Kalini's shoulder.

Kalini sat up. "I was having an awful dream. Thunder was calling me, he needed me . . . "

"I think something's wrong. We need to go to the stables!" Amara whispered.

Kalini didn't hesitate. They threw on their clothes and crept out of the house. Amara had told her parents that she'd be going to the stables very early, so she knew they wouldn't worry when they got up and found that she and Kalini had already left.

They ran down the lane, stumbling over

potholes in the grey half-light. Another bolt of lightning shot down from the sky, its blazing white point shooting directly towards the stables. There was a loud bang and Amara's heart somersaulted in her chest. "What was that?" she said, stopping.

"Look!" gasped Kalini, pointing.

They both stared in horror as they saw the orange glow of flames lighting up the grey sky right above the stables.

"The stables are on fire!" Amara cried.

They sprinted on. Rounding the corner towards the stables, they heard the clatter of hooves, and a bay horse with a black mane and tail crackling with electricity came galloping out of the driveway. Its hooves sent up a spray of stones as it turned and raced towards the woods at the end of the lane.

Amara recognised the horse instantly – and
the dark-haired, pale-faced rider urging it on.

"It's Bolt and Ivy!" she cried.

In her elemental form, Bolt was able to

gallop far faster than any normal horse and in seconds she had reached the woods and disappeared into the trees.

"Amara! Quick!" Kalini shouted, tugging Amara's arm.

They raced up the driveway and clambered over the gate.

"Look at this place!" Kalini gasped. The yard – so beautifully clean and tidy when they had left it the evening before – had been trashed. Mud had been kicked over the newly painted stable doors; the plant pots and hanging baskets had been turned upside down, soil and broken plants spilling out from them; forks, brooms and wheelbarrows had been blown over and buckets were rolling round on their sides. Amara hardly stopped to take it all in – her eyes were on the barn near the Meadow Stable block where the bales of hay and straw were kept. She could see there was a jagged hole in the roof and flames were leaping up from inside.

Jill was hobbling towards the fire, a hosepipe in her hand. Amara could hear frantic whinnying coming from the Meadow Stables.

"We need to get the horses!" Amara shouted to Kalini. "They can help!"

Heart hammering in her chest, she ran faster than she had ever run in her life. "The barn's on fire!" Amara yelled, sliding back the stable bolts and flinging open the doors of the Meadow Stables.

The elemental horses galloped out. Tide and Cloud transformed into their true form, their grey coats turning a pale silvery blue and their manes and tails swirling like frothing white sea foam. Elemental horses' magic was always at its strongest when they were in their magical form.

In the blink of an eye, they had reached the barn. Cloud reared up and a heavy grey rain cloud instantly materialised. Rain cascaded through the hole in the roof, dousing the fire below.

Tide set to work too. Turning to the nearby trough, she stamped her front hooves. The water in the trough swirled upwards, obeying her command. Tide directed it in through the barn door in a fierce jet, putting out the flames that the rain wasn't reaching. Thick smoke billowed out, making them all cough.

"Well done!" Amara heard Jill shout to Tide and Cloud.

The two water horses transformed back and stood, panting, tired from doing the magic.

Sirocco and Thunder reached them and conjured a wind to blow the smoke away.

Suddenly, Amara heard Ember whinny.

Amara! The stable roof!

Swinging round, she realised that some sparks from the barn's fire had fallen on the plants covering the roof of Meadow Stables. The creepers that had been there longest were drying out and as the sparks fell on them, they started to smoulder. The wind now sweeping over them was fanning the flames. Amara raced to the hosepipe on the wall of the stable block and frantically turned the tap on as far as it would go, the metal slipping in her impatient fingers. She knew that if the fire caught hold of the roof the whole stable block would be in danger of burning down!

She aimed the hosepipe up at the flames but the jet of water wasn't powerful enough – the water only just reached the guttering, splattering down on to the ground. The flames were starting to spread. "Help!" she yelled frantically. "Over here! The stable roof's on fire!"

There was a whinny and the clatter of hooves. Glancing round, she expected to see Cloud or Tide but it was Rose, now in her true form. Her eyes glowed with a silvery light and her usually flaxen mane and tail were a mossy green, filled with wildflowers. She stamped her hooves and almost instantly a thick new wave of creepers swept across the roof like a heavy blanket, smothering the flames.

Amara felt a tidal wave of relief. "Thank you, Rose!" she gasped as Rose changed back into her pony form. Amara threw her arms round her neck and Rose staggered.

"Rose? Are you OK?" Amara demanded.

Rose's sides were heaving as if she'd just galloped ten miles. Her legs trembled and she sank to the ground. With a groan, she collapsed on to her side.

"Jill!" Amara shrieked. "Come quick!"

CHAPTER EIGHT

Jill crouched beside the chestnut pony, checking her pulse by pressing two fingers under Rose's jaw. Kalini had reached Amara and they were holding hands tightly. The other ponies had gathered around them and were watching anxiously.

To Amara's intense relief, Rose lifted her head.

"Is she going to be OK?" Amara breathed, her throat dry.

Jill's face was creased with worry. "She's very sick. That last piece of magic used up all her energy and strength."

"Rose!" They heard a horrified cry and glanced round to see Alex sprinting across the yard towards them, Imogen hot on his heels. "What's happened to her?" Alex cried, throwing himself on the ground beside his horse. With an effort, Rose lifted her muzzle and placed it on his knees. He touched her forehead, his eyes filling with tears. "Rose. Oh, Rose," he said, stroking her face.

Amara swallowed, her eyes prickling. For all Alex's wild energy and impulsiveness, his tactlessness and temper, she knew he loved Rose deeply and she could only imagine how awful it must be for him to see her looking so weak.

"I think she'll be OK, Alex," said Jill, putting her hand on his shoulder. "She's just very, very tired now. She used her last bit of magic to save the stable roof but at the next full moon she can renew her magic and strength."

"But that's not for weeks," said Alex. "We've got to do something to help her!"

Amara remembered something Jill had said. "What about that spring you told us about? You said its water can strengthen an elemental horse's magic. Can we fetch some water from it and bring it back for Rose to drink?"

Jill shook her head. "It wouldn't help. It only properly renews an elemental horse if they drink from the source of the spring themselves."

"I'll take Rose there then!" said Alex.

"It's a three hour ride, Alex," said Jill. "I doubt Rose would make it and even if she managed it, the spring is halfway down a cliff and really dangerous to get to."

Tide and Thunder whinnied and Ember stepped forward. He nudged Amara's shoulder. *We can go with Rose and Alex. We can help them and make sure they get there and get down to the spring safely.*

Amara told Jill what he'd said.

Kalini nodded. "Thunder's saying the same thing."

"And Tide," said Imogen.

Rose whickered faintly.

"She's saying that with the others' help she thinks she'll be able to reach the spring, Jill," said Alex.

Jill considered it for a moment and then came to a decision. "OK then, you can go." She glanced round. "With the yard in this state, I'll have to cancel the open afternoon anyway."

"What happened?" asked Imogen, looking at the smoking stable roof, the damaged barn and the chaos on the yard.

"It was Ivy and Bolt," Jill said grimly. "They came to the yard at dawn. I was asleep and didn't hear Bolt at first. I only woke up when I heard the ponies whinnying." She gestured to the protective boot on her injured ankle. "It takes me a while to get up and put my boot on so I can walk. By the time I got out on the yard the place was in chaos and Bolt's lightning had hit the barn."

"But why would Ivy do this?" said Imogen,

sweeping her arm around.

"Because she wanted to wreck our open afternoon," guessed Amara, remembering the way Ivy had torn down their poster the day before.

"And wanted to cause so much damage there'd be no way I could afford to keep Moonlight Stables open," said Jill.

"But why?" said Kalini, looking bemused. "Storm Stables is really successful. Ivy doesn't need to shut Moonlight Stables down."

"It's more than just a business issue. Ivy hates me," said Jill. "We grew up together and we were friends – best friends – but then," she shook her head, her eyes clouding with memories, "we both became True Riders and that's when the trouble started.

My horse, Shula . . . " Her voice trembled slightly as she spoke her horse's name. "She was an incredibly powerful Fire Horse. Bolt didn't have nearly as much power back then. Ivy was jealous and, well, things happened. Things I can never forgive her for." She swallowed. "Ivy became a Night Rider and has hated me ever since. The more trouble she can cause the better as far as she is concerned." She looked around and heaved a sigh. "Maybe this time she's won."

"No!" Amara exclaimed. "We won't let her!"

"But I've got no way of paying for repairs to the barn or the stables," said Jill wearily. "The open afternoon was my last hope."

"It can still go ahead," said Amara, thinking fast. "Everyone's coming to practise the ride in a few hours. We could ring them and ask them to come early and help tidy."

"But what about the ride?" said Jill. "The four of you won't be here."

"Bea knows the display. She can teach it to Jasmine and Ollie and they'll be able to help her get the younger ones to practise," said Imogen quickly.

Amara nodded. "Even if it's not as good as it was going to be, people will still like watching it."

A smile spread across Jill's face. "OK. I'll see what can be done but you four must concentrate on Rose. Nothing matters more than helping her get her strength back. Agreed?"

"Agreed!" they all chorused.

Half an hour later, everyone who rode at Moonlight Stables had been called or messaged and nearly all of them had agreed to come and help. Ollie, Jasmine and Bea arrived and after hearing the plan, they set to work cleaning up.

"Don't worry about anything," Jasmine said. She ran a hand through her dark hair. "Though how we're going to get this place fit for visitors this afternoon, I have no idea!"

Amara and the others were just about to set off when Malia walked through the gate.

She looked round at the mess, her eyes widening. "What's happened?"

Amara didn't know what to say. "It was ... um ... "

"Vandals," said Imogen quickly.

"Vandals?" Malia echoed. "That's awful!"

They nodded.

"We've got to go out now," said Amara. "Rose isn't very well and we have to fetch her some medicine."

"Can't the vet come here?" said Malia in surprise.

"Not right now," said Amara. "We might be out for some time."

"If you don't mind helping the others to clear up a bit and get the riding school ponies ready, that would be great," said Imogen. "We're still going ahead with the open afternoon."

"We need to have it more than ever," said Kalini. "Lightning struck the barn and there was a fire."

Malia looked horrified. "Oh no. Of course I'll help. You go and get Rose's medicine. She really doesn't look well."

Amara and the others rode slowly into the woods and up to the ridgeway. From there, they would head along bridlepaths until they reached Magpie Hill, where the spring was. Jill had written the directions down and shown them where they were going on a map.

Usually when they went out into the countryside they cantered but now they stuck to walking and trotting, not wanting to tire Rose out. However, despite the slower pace, after an hour Rose started to stumble and lag behind. Alex jumped off. "I'll walk the rest of the way," he called. "She's very tired."

Without Alex on her back, Rose was able to go faster. Alex jogged beside her but the ground was rough and he kept tripping over stones and having to dodge round rabbit holes.

"Tide says you can ride with me," said Imogen, turning round.

"It's OK," said Alex. "I can manage." As if to prove it, he jumped over a rabbit hole but as he did so, he caught the toe of his trainer in a tuft of long grass. When he landed, he sprawled on to the ground.

"Ow!" he gasped, his hands going to his left ankle.

"Are you all right?" said Kalini in alarm.

"Yeah," he said, wincing in pain and getting to his feet. "I've just twisted my ankle; it'll be fine. I don't need any help." He started to hobble up the slope.

"Alex, stop being dumb!" Imogen exclaimed in exasperation. "Rose needs us to get to the spring as quickly as possible. You're not helping her by insisting on walking. Just ride Tide with me."

For a moment, Amara thought Alex was going to argue but then he nodded. "OK. Thanks," he muttered to Imogen. Taking her outstretched hand, he vaulted up behind her.

With Alex now on Tide, they were able to go at a much faster pace but it still seemed ages before they got to Magpie Hill.

We're not going to get back in time for the display, are we? Amara said to Ember.

There's still a chance, he replied hopefully.

Amara hung on to that faint hope but when they found the spring, her hopes

faded. It was halfway down a very steep slope. It bubbled out of the rocky ground and then twisted away in a sparkling, bubbling stream that fell into the rocky ravine below.

"How's Rose going to get down there?" she said, looking at the steep slope.

Rose was puffing hard but she walked to the lip of the slope.

"She says she'll try," said Alex, jumping off Tide and limping over to Rose. He stroked her face. "You can do this, girl."

Rose cautiously stepped on to the slope, leaning back to keep her balance as she edged downwards but the strain was too much for her. Her legs started to shake and she stopped.

The other ponies whinnied encouragingly. Amara could feel anxiety surging through

Ember. She could tell he was as worried as she was.

"Come on, Rose. It's just a little further and then you'll be by the spring!" urged Alex.

Rose took another cautious step forward but then both her hind legs slipped underneath her and she fell heavily on to her side, slipping down the slope and coming to a halt. "Rose!" exclaimed Alex, ignoring his injured ankle and scrambling down the slope, holding on to tufts of grass to prevent himself from falling. He stopped beside her. Rose was panting hard.

"She says she can't get up!" Alex shouted to the others. "I need help!"

We have to do something! Ember said to Amara.

Amara's mouth felt dry as she looked at

Rose stuck on the steep slope. Ember was right. But what could they do? How could they possibly get Rose back on her feet? The slope was so steep and she was much too heavy for them to lift.

Suddenly, Imogen gasped. "Didn't Jill say that a horse had to drink from the source of the spring in order for their strength to be fully restored?" Amara and Kalini nodded. "Well, Rose doesn't need her magic to be *fully* restored – right now she just needs enough strength so that she can get down to the spring and drink by herself. Tide, could you use your magic to get some of the water from the spring up to Alex and Rose and see if that helps?"

Tide nodded quickly, and turning towards the stream, she stamped her hoof. A narrow stream of water spiralled upwards from the spring and arched towards Rose. It sprinkled down around her in gentle drops. She blinked and opened her eyes, lifting her head.

"Catch the water, Alex, then she'll be able to drink it!" Imogen shouted.

Alex realised what she meant and held his hands out. The water puddled inside his cupped hands and he offered it to Rose.

The chestnut pony drank. Alex repeated the process. As Rose lifted her nose from his hands for the second time, Amara noticed something. "Her eyes are looking brighter! Keep going!"

Alex collected more water in his hands and after the fifth time of drinking, Rose lifted her head properly. Water droplets were streaking down her coat, plastering her forelock to her face, but she looked much brighter. Pushing her front legs out, she scrambled to her feet and Tide stopped using her magic.

"I hope she can get down to the spring OK," said Amara anxiously. Although Rose looked better, she didn't look completely steady on her feet.

Thunder and I can help her get there

safely, Ember said. *Jump off, Amara.*

Amara did as he asked. "Be careful!" she called anxiously as he and Thunder edged carefully down the steep slope, pebbles rolling away from under their hooves, skittering down into the ravine at the bottom. Amara didn't like to think what would happen if either of the horses fell. But they were both strong and sure-footed.

They made their way over to Rose and then pressed close on either side of her, supporting her as she made her way carefully down the slope on shaky legs. "That's it! Good girl, Rose. You're almost there!" Alex encouraged, starting to climb back to the others.

"Go on, Thunder! Go on, Ember!" called Kalini and Amara.

"You'll be there any second," called Imogen, and Tide whinnied too.

The horses reached the spring. Rose sank to her knees on her front legs and, pushing her muzzle into the bubbling water, she drank deeply. First her legs stopped trembling, then her coat started to shine, her eyes began to sparkle and when she finally lifted her head and stood up, she looked just like her old self. Better even – she suddenly looked as if she was bursting with energy. With a delighted whinny, she shook her mane, spun round and galloped confidently up the stony slope. Thunder and Ember followed. They leapt over the lip of the slope, on to the flat ground where the girls and Alex were standing, whinnying in delight.

"Rose says thank you to everyone!" said

Alex, beaming as he hugged her.

"I'm so glad she's OK," said Amara, breathing out in a rush of relief.

"All of your horses were awesome," said Alex. He gave the girls a slightly sheepish grin. "You too. Thanks for helping."

"See, sometimes you do need to let your friends help," said Imogen, going over and giving him a hug.

"I guess so," he muttered.

"That's not enough, doughnut brain," said Imogen, shaking her head at him. "I want to hear you say, *You were right, Immy. Sometimes I need help.*"

"You were right, Immy," Alex echoed, rolling his eyes. "Sometimes I need help."

Amara smiled. "We all do!"

Alex vaulted on to Rose. "OK, enough with

the talking! We've got a display to do!"

"We'll never make it," said Kalini.

"We will if we use . . . " Alex paused, saying something to Rose. She whinnied in delight and transformed into her magical form.

"Elemental magic!" gasped the girls.

"Yep!" said Alex with a grin.

In an instant, Ember, Tide and Thunder had transformed too. They galloped away across the hillside, moving far faster than normal horses. Amara's heart raced as Ember's mane – now magical golden flickering flames – billowed around her. She could feel her whole body sparkling with magic as Ember used his powers. His hooves pounded on the grass, his strides eating up the miles. Would they get back in time? And what state would the yard be in when they got there? Now Rose was safe there was just one thought beating through her mind – they had to save Moonlight Stables!

CHAPTER NINE

When they reached the woods, the horses changed back to their pony form. Cantering out of the trees at the bottom of the lane, they skidded to a stop in surprise. There were cars lining both sides of the usually empty lane.

"It looks like plenty of people have come," said Amara.

"I hope the others managed to make the yard look OK," said Imogen.

Ember trotted towards the driveway, his black ears pricked. The sound of voices and laughter filled the air. The gate was open and as they rode on to the yard, Amara caught her breath.

"Oh, wow!" Kalini breathed. "Look!" The yard looked just as neat as it had done the evening before. The plant pots and baskets were brimming with flowers and the stable doors were bright and clean. Someone had strung pastel bunting up and it waved

merrily in the breeze. Children were pulling their parents around by the hands, dragging them over to pat the friendly riding school ponies over their stable doors.

"I'll go find Jill and tell her Rose is better," said Alex, riding off.

Jasmine and a group of her school friends were painting faces and braiding hair. Bea's mum and dad were selling drinks and a couple of other parents were selling bags of fertiliser. Ollie was busy with his cake stall.

People were putting money into a big bucket labelled *DONATIONS TO SAVE OUR STABLES! THANK YOU!*

"How did the others do all this?" said Imogen.

"I have no idea," said Amara in astonishment.

"Amara!" Amara looked round and saw Malia hurrying through the crowd. "How's Rose?" Her eyes widened as she caught sight of Alex riding away. "Wow! She's looking so much better."

"Yes, she's fine now," said Amara.

"That's brilliant! And what do you think about this?" said Malia, gesturing round. "Isn't it great?"

"I'll tell you who's great," said Jasmine, reaching them and flinging an arm round

Malia's shoulder. "Malia! She's been amazing!"

Malia blushed. "I haven't."

"Don't listen to her," Jasmine told the others. "She's totally awesome. She worked so hard helping us clean up the yard and she was brilliant when it came to the display. She rearranged things, pairing all the younger ones with someone older so they don't have to remember everything on their own. She even got them all cleaning the tack and grooming the ponies after the practice."

"It wasn't that big a deal," said Malia modestly.

"Malia!" Cleo and Taylor came skipping through the crowd together. They each grabbed Malia's hands. "Come and see how clean the bridles are now."

"And we've put ribbons in the ponies' manes!" said Taylor.

"See you later!" Malia called to Amara and the others as the younger girls dragged her off.

"Wow," said Amara, looking at Jasmine. "She's always seemed so shy before."

"She definitely wasn't shy when she was organising the display," said Jasmine.

"I'm so glad it's sorted. I still don't understand how you managed to tidy up the yard so well though," said Imogen.

Jasmine grinned and leaned closer. "There may have been a bit of magic involved when people weren't looking," she whispered. "Cloud made it rain to clean the yard, Sirocco and Sparks dried everywhere off, Sandy covered the burns on the barn floor with sand. And Forest helped too. You know he usually can't control his earth magic?" They nodded. "Well, today, for the first time, he managed to grow flowers. He filled all the plant pots and hanging baskets. Anyway," She checked her watch. "The display is due to start in half an hour. Are you going to take part?"

Do you want to, Ember? Amara asked.

Definitely! he said.

"Ember and I will," Amara said out loud.

"And me and Thunder," said Kalini.

Imogen nodded too. "Tide wants to as well."

"Then go and get ready!" said Jasmine, looking at the ponies' muddy legs. "There's no time to waste!"

Half an hour later, everyone gathered to watch the display. The ponies' coats shone, their tails were tangle-free, hoof oil made their hooves sparkle and the smaller riding school ponies all had bright ribbons plaited into their manes. The plaits were wonky but their riders looked so pleased with themselves that it didn't matter at all.

Amara could feel Ember's excitement – he loved any chance to show off! Her stomach felt like it was tying itself in knots. The open afternoon had gone really well so far – if they could manage to do an impressive display then maybe Jill would get the donations and new clients she needed to do the repairs and keep Moonlight Stables open.

She saw Jill speaking to Malia and her mum. "We may not be the smartest riding school but I am so proud of the children who ride here," she was saying. "The older ones especially. I'd been thinking about shutting down after the winter we've had – no indoor school means no lessons when the weather's bad. Ever since they heard that, they've worked tirelessly to try and fundraise to help me out. They're a great group of kids." She smiled. "I guess you must be used to far smarter yards than this."

"When I was growing up, I used to help at a riding school very similar to this one," said Malia's mum. "I had some great times there." She smiled at the memory.

"Malia! Malia!" Nikita called. "Please can you tighten Pepper's girth?"

"Malia! I've forgotten what we do after we trot a twenty-metre circle," shouted Josh.

"Malia, could you grab my water bottle, please?" Jasmine asked. "It's just on the fence but I can't reach it."

Malia left her mum and ran to help.

Her mum shook her head. "I can't quite believe how comfortable Malia is down here," she confided in Jill. "She suffers from social anxiety and she usually finds it very hard to make friends."

"Well, she hasn't had a problem here," said Jill as Malia busied herself with helping everyone. "She's a lovely girl. Any time she wants to come and help she'll be very welcome. Now, let's get this display started!"

She opened the gate and let the ponies in. The riders got into their pairs, a younger one with an older rider apart from Amara and Imogen, who were the lead pair. Jill picked up a megaphone and called for quiet. "There will now be a musical display," she announced. "The students have organised this all on their own and I'm hugely proud of them. Please put your hands together for the riders of Moonlight Stables!"

Everyone clapped. Alex was sitting at the edge of the school. He pressed play and the introductory music blasted out of the speakers he'd set up. Amara and Imogen clicked their tongues and Ember and Tide moved into a trot. They all trotted round the school, the pairs spaced out neatly.

"Aw! Look at those little ones!" Amara heard people in the crowd saying as Cleo, Josh, Nikita and Taylor trotted past.

As Amara rode past the fence at the bottom where people were watching, her heart plummeted. Zara, Daniela and Shannon! They were standing at the end of the row near where the spare bags of fertiliser had been stacked.

"What are they doing here?" Amara hissed to Imogen.

"I have no idea," said Imogen, staring at the Storm Stables girls, who were leaning against the top bar of the fence. When they saw Amara and Imogen looking at them, they smirked. Amara groaned inwardly. She was sure they were up to something.

Trying hard to ignore them, she glanced at Imogen. "Ready?"

"Ready!" said Imogen.

There was no time to be anxious. Forcing

big smiles on to their faces, they turned
down the centre line and the display began!

CHAPTER TEN

The other riders followed Amara and Imogen down the centre line in their pairs. As they all halted, Amara could hear the little ones talking to their ponies.

"Good girl, Pepper!"

"You're the best, Blue!

"Come on, Pips, we can do this!"

She smiled and she and Imogen led off again at a trot. Reaching the gate, she went left and Imogen went right. As Ember turned, Shannon suddenly leant over the fence and opened an umbrella. Ember instinctively tensed, his head shooting up. Ponies – even super clever magical ones – hated sudden movements and noises. *It's OK,* she told him. *It's just an umbrella.*

To her relief, he recovered himself and led the other ponies past Shannon and the umbrella as if there was nothing there.

The riders circled and changed the rein, moved across the school and rode a figure of eight. It was all going well when Amara suddenly heard a loud clatter. Swinging round, she saw that Daniela had dropped a grooming kit just as some of the little ones were riding past.

"Whoopsie!" she said as Pepper and Blue both jumped in surprise. A few of the people in the crowd gave her annoyed looks.

Luckily the younger children kept their heads. They all patted their ponies and reassured them, and the ride carried on, the ponies criss-crossing the school and meeting in pairs and fours. But Amara felt tense and she kept glancing over at the Storm Stables girls. Did they have anything else planned?

As Cleo, the youngest rider, rode past them on Pippin the Shetland pony, Amara saw Zara pull a fluorescent jacket out of her bag and flap it.

Pippin shied. The crowd gasped as Cleo lurched to one side but she pulled herself back into the saddle and patted Pippin's neck. "It's OK, good boy. Don't be scared," she soothed. She held up her hand and Alex stopped the music.

Cleo rode over to Zara. "Please don't do that," she said in a clear, polite voice. "You might not know much about ponies, but they get scared of things that flap."

There was a moment's shocked silence and then the crowd all clapped, their faces breaking into wide smiles. Cleo nodded to Alex, he started the music again and she rode back to join Bea.

Blushing like a tomato, Zara shoved the jacket in her bag and muttered something to the other two girls. They turned to leave but just as they did so, a sudden strong gust of wind seemed to blow out of nowhere. It swept across the school and hit the bags of fertiliser, making the top one fall from the pile. It hit the ground with a thud and burst open, spraying fertiliser over Zara, Daniela and Shannon's shoes.

They shrieked in disgust.

Amara had to bite her tongue to stop herself from laughing as she saw them stomp off. Glancing round, she saw Kalini looking rather shocked and Thunder looking very smug.

Go, Thunder! Ember said to her.

Amara grinned.

The team finished the display, the younger ones trotting round in single file while the older ones weaved in and out of them at a canter before they all came together again and halted in the centre in a straight line. It had gone perfectly!

The audience clapped and cheered as they bowed and then Alex opened the gate and they all rode out of the school, patting their ponies. Amara felt a mixture of satisfaction and worry. It was such a relief that the ride had gone well but had they done enough to save the stables?

"The ride was great!" Malia said, patting Ember.

"Thanks for helping," said Amara. "It was

a great idea to pair the younger riders with older ones."

"No problem," said Malia, smiling and shrugging.

"You all did really well," said Jill, coming over with Malia's mum.

"Absolutely," said Malia's mum. "Everyone obviously has a great time here. It reminds me of the fun I had when I was at a riding school." She glanced at her daughter. "I'd love Malia to experience it too, so I've decided to make a donation to your fund."

She pulled a cheque book out of her pocket, wrote a cheque and handed it to Jill.

Jill stared at the figure on the cheque, wide eyed. "But this is so much money. I can't possibly accept it."

"Please do," Malia's mum said. "Nothing

matters more to me than Malia's happiness and it's very clear she isn't happy at Storm Stables. Everything I've seen today has made me believe that this would be a much better place for her, provided she is able to ride all year round – please see my donation as my way of making that happen. You can use the money to build an indoor school."

"Oh my goodness!" Jill looked overwhelmed. "With an indoor school I can teach all year and I won't have to think about closing."

Amara and the others exchanged delighted looks.

Malia hugged her mum. "Oh, thank you! Thank you! Thank you!"

"You're going to be a Moonlight Stables rider," Amara told her.

Malia beamed. "I can't wait!"

"Everything's worked out so perfectly!" said Imogen later that afternoon as the ponies grazed in the meadow while the sun sank down into the horizon. They were all riding bareback with just headcollars on. Amara didn't think she'd ever felt more tired – or more happy.

After the open afternoon had ended, Jill had counted the money and discovered that along with Malia's mum's donation she now had enough to repair the tack room as well as the Meadow Stables and the barn, and she could replace the hay and straw that had been burned in the fire. Lots of new clients had signed up for lessons – so many that Jill had even said she might have to think about buying a couple of new ponies!

"We did it," said Kalini. "We saved Moonlight Stables."

"And we saved Rose," said Alex, bending down to hug Rose's neck.

The chestnut pony snorted gratefully.

"I'm so glad Malia doesn't have to stay at Storm Stables any longer!" said Amara.

"Do you think she might be a True Rider?" Kalini asked.

Imogen looked thoughtful. "I don't know. Remember that Jasmine said Forest suddenly managed to control his magic today? It could just have been a coincidence but maybe it was because Malia was here."

"I hope she is a True Rider," said Amara. "But even if she isn't, I bet she's going to be happy here."

"A lot happier than at Storm Stables!" said Alex. He chuckled. "It was very funny when that fertiliser spilt all over Zara, Shannon and Daniela's shoes, wasn't it?"

"I had to try so hard not to laugh. Did you see their faces?" said Imogen.

"Serves them right for trying to sabotage us!" said Amara.

They continued to talk about the day until the sun had set and it was time to take the ponies in. As they rode back to the stables together, Amara felt overwhelmed by happiness. *Oh, Ember, being a True Rider at Moonlight Stables is the best thing ever!*

Ember snorted. *No, having you as my True Rider is the best thing ever, Amara.*

Amara hugged him and smiled.

Have you read the first Moonlight
Riders book ...
FIRE HORSE
Read on for a sneak peek!

Amara cantered along the narrow lane. The
sun was shining and the yellow daffodils in
the hedgerow were nodding their heads in
the spring breeze. Amara slowed to a trot
as she rounded the bend. She straightened
her back, remembering what she had read
about good riding, and set off once more.
Amara wasn't riding a real horse, she was
on her own two feet, but in her imagination
she was mounted on a beautiful black pony
with a white star called Midnight. She leapt
over a puddle, imagining they were soaring
over a jump. With her two long brown plaits
bouncing on her shoulders, she cantered
around a bend in the lane and then stopped.

On the left-hand side there was a riding stables. A driveway led up a slope, past a bungalow with a pretty front garden, to a metal gate. Beyond the gate, Amara could see a stable block with each of the doors painted a different colour. A sign read *Moonlight Stables,* and underneath were the words *Proprietor: Jill Reed.*

The Easter holidays had just started and Amara's parents had said it was OK for her to ask if the riding school needed any help, but now she was actually there, she could feel her tummy twisting into nervous knots. Maybe she wouldn't go in after all.

To be continued . . .

True Rider: Amara Thompson

Age:
10

Appearance:
Brown hair and blue eyes

Lives with:
Parents

Best friend:
Kalini

Favourite things to do:
Anything with horses, drawing and reading pony stories

Favourite mounted game:
Bending race

I most want to improve:
Vaulting on and off at speed and getting my handovers right

Elemental Horse: Ember

Colour:
Black

Height:
14.1hh

Personality:
Loving, lively, hot-tempered

Pony breed:
Welsh section B x Thoroughbred

Elemental appearance:
Golden eyes, swirling mane and a magical, fiery tail

Elemental abilities:
Fire Horse - Ember can create fires, make things burst into flame and cast fire balls from his hooves

True Rider: Imogen Fairfax

Age:
10

Appearance:
Light brown hair and hazel eyes

Lives with:
Mum, Dad, two brothers Will (17)
and Tim (15), Minnie our cockapoo

Best friend:
Alex

Favourite things to do:
Anything with horses, walking
Minnie, helping at my gran's
teashop

Favourite mounted game:
Mug shuffle

I most want to improve:
My accuracy in races

Elemental Horse: Tide

Colour:
White-grey

Height:
14.1hh

Personality:
Thoughtful, sensitive and kind

Pony breed:
Arab x Welsh

Elemental appearance:
Blue eyes, silver-blue coat and a
flowing sea foam mane and tail

Elemental abilities:
Water Horse - Tide can make
it rain and manipulate bodies
of water to create waves,
whirlpools and waterspouts

True Rider: Alex Brahler

Age:
11

Appearance:
Black hair and dark brown eyes

Lives with:
Mum, Dad, sister Frankie
(15) and our chocolate Labradors,
Scooby and Murphy

Best friend:
Imogen

Favourite things to do:
Anything with horses, playing
football, cross-country running,
climbing and swimming

Favourite mounted game:
Five-flag race

I most want to improve:
Being more patient in
competitions so I'm not
eliminated by starting races
before the flag falls!

Elemental Horse: Rose

Colour:
Bright chestnut with flaxen
mane and tail, a white blaze
and four white socks

Height:
14.2 hh

Personality:
Patient, calm, confident

Pony Breed:
Welsh section C

Elemental appearance:
Bright green eyes, a mossy green
mane and tail covered in flowers

Elemental abilities:
Earth Horse - Rose can make plants
and flowers grow

Night Rider: Zara Watson

Age:
II

Appearance:
Blonde hair and green eyes

Lives with:
Mum most of the time
and Dad some of the time

Best friend:
Daniela (my cousin)

Favourite things to do:
Riding, playing tennis, shopping,
pamper sessions

Favourite mounted game:
Bottle race

I most want to improve:
Nothing, I'm good at everything

Elemental Horse: Scorch

Colour:
Bright chestnut with a white blaze

Height:
14.2hh

Personality:
Lively, mean, impatient

Pony Breed:
Show Pony x Thoroughbred

Elemental appearance:
Red eyes, mane and tail of dark
flickering flames

Elemental abilities:
Fire Horse - although not as
powerful as Ember, Scorch can heat
things up and cause small fires

Moonlight Riders

Meet all the True Riders of Moonlight Stables and their amazing elemental horses!

Moonlight Riders

Sea Foal

LINDA CHAPMAN

Do you have what it takes to become a True Rider?